Dance Together Dinosaurs

DANCE TOGETHER DINOSAURS
A RED FOX BOOK 978 1 782 95558 0

Published in Great Britain by Red Fox,
an imprint of Random House Children's Books
A Random House Group Company
This edition published 2012

1 3 5 7 9 10 8 6 4 2

Text copyright © Jane Clarke, 2012
Illustrations copyright © Lee Wildish, 2012

The right of Jane Clarke and Lee Wildish to be identified
as the author and illustrator of this work has been asserted in accordance
with the Copyright, Design and Patents Act 1988.

Red Fox Books are published by Random House Children's Books,
61–63 Uxbridge Road, London W5 5SA

www.randomhouse.co.uk
www.kidsatrandomhouse.co.uk

Addresses for companies within The Random House Group Limited
can be found at: www.randomhouse.co.uk/offices.htm

THE RANDOM HOUSE GROUP Limited Reg. No. 954009
A CIP catalogue record for this book is available from the British Library.

Printed in China

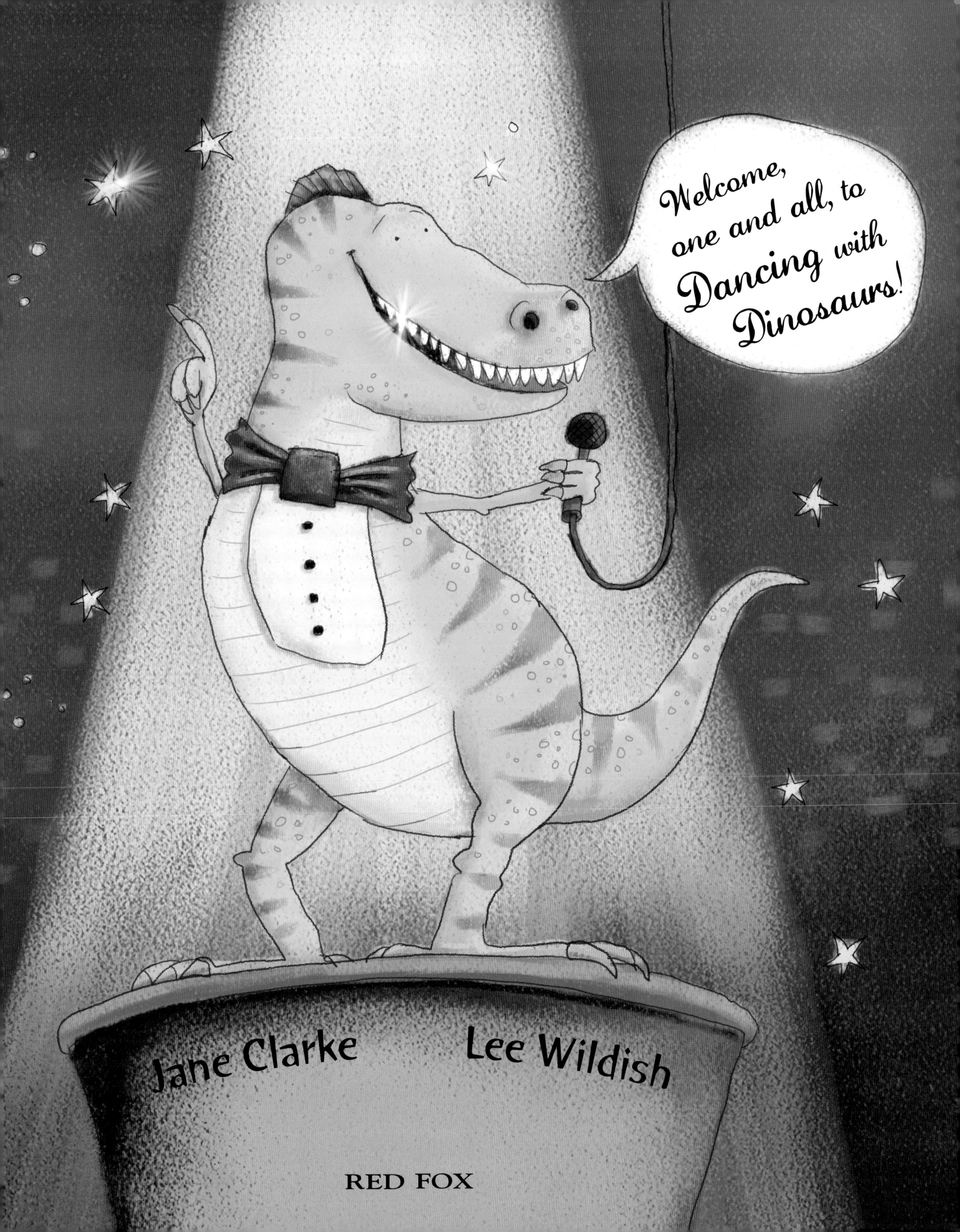

Jane Clarke
Lee Wildish

RED FOX

Meet the contestants!

Our fang-tastic tyrannosaurus, T. Rex

Steggy Stegosaurus, our diamond-plated dancer

The Hadrosaur Duckbills are everything they're quacked-up to be

Be filled with rapture watching the raptor

Troodie is a truly talented troodon

Patty Apatosaurus is a whole heap of fun

Dancing
comes tops with
Tracey Triceratops

Barry
Baryonyx
is clawsome

Kylie
Ankylosaurus
loves to dance when
she's out clubbing

Maia
Maiasaurus is over the
moon to be taking part

Donny
Iguanodon gives
dancing a thumbs-up

Spike
Spinosaurus sticks
out from the crowd

Lily Dilophosaurus is
frilled to take part

Head bang with
Pachycephalosaurus and
the Bone-head Breakers

Dinosaurs, get ready!
Polish your fangs and claws,
don't keep the judges waiting–
come dancing with the 'saurs!

Tango with our T. Rex,

do the **Steggy** twist and **shout!**

Disco with the Duckbills

and shake it all about.

Tap along with raptors,

do the **Troodie boogaloo,**

stomp
a 'saurus samba

round Patty's pile of poo.

Body pop with Tracey Tops,

be swayed by **Barry's rumba,**

Cha-cha-cha with Kylie

in her great **big** sparkly number.

Moonwalk with Miss Maia,

step a Spike o'saurus jig,

put on your cowboy boots and hat,

line up with Donny Ig.

Get down
with the Breakers,

waltz along with Lily,

join the **All-saur All-stars** ballet

wearing tights and something frilly.

It's tons of fun for everyone,
until it's time . . .

JUDGES

...for dinner!